This book belongs to:

....

Inspired by Agnese - CS
For Honey Blossom - F.E.

This edition first published in 2020 by Alligator Products Ltd.
Cupcake is an imprint of Alligator Products Ltd
2nd Floor, 314 Regents Park Road, London N3 2JX

www.alligatorbooks.co.uk

Written by Christine Swift
Illustrated by Frank Endersby

Printed in China.1567

Little Bird
Finds Her Voice

cupcake

Little Bird loved the garden.

The other birds sang beautiful songs whilst they splashed in the water.

Little Bird wanted to sing, but she was too shy.

As the other birds flew away, Little Bird was left behind.
She couldn't even tweet to ask them to wait!

Little Bird thought she saw another bird, so she flew towards it.

Soon Little Bird realised that she had made a mistake.

In the shadows, she saw something slowly creeping towards her!

Little Bird was frightened.

Where could she hide?

Little Bird flew up to a shelf and hid between some books.

Looking down, Little Bird could see a cat sitting, watching her.

Outside, the sun was setting.

Little Bird was tired
and soon fell asleep.

Little Bird was woken by the noise from the birds outside in the garden.

They had returned and were singing beautiful morning songs.

Little Bird wanted to be outside with them in the garden.

She peeped down and saw that the cat was still there!

Little Bird tried very hard to call for help.

To Little Bird's surprise, she sang the most beautiful song!

The cat tilted his head to listen, he loved her song!

Little Bird sang again.

Then Little Bird looked down at the cat. He seemed friendly.

The cat looked up at Little Bird.

Suddenly the cat jumped onto the back of a chair.

"Miaow," he said.

Little Bird was scared, but she followed the cat as he led her safely to the window!

Little Bird could hear her friends.

Soon she could see her friends through the window!

As she flew outside, Little Bird sang a very beautiful "Thank you" to the kind cat.

Back in the garden, Little Bird was so happy,
she sang to her heart's content.

Little Bird had found her voice, and what a wonderful
voice it was!

The end